Richmal Crompton, who wrote the original *Just William* stories, was born in Lancashire in 1890. The first story about William Brown appeared in *Home* magazine in 1919, and the first collection of William stories was published in book form three years later. In all, thirty-eight William books were published, the last one in 1970, after Richmal Crompton's death.

Martin Jarvis, who has adapted the stories in this book for younger readers, first discovered *Just William* when he was nine years old. He made his first adaptation of a William story for BBC radio in 1973 and since then his broadcast readings have become classics in their own right. BBC Worldwide have released nearly a hundred William stories on audio cassette and for these international best-sellers Martin has received a Gold Disc and the British Talkies Award. An award-winning actor, Martin has also appeared in numerous stage plays, television series and films.

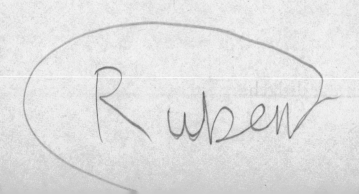

Titles in the *Meet Just William* series

All *Meet Just William* titles can be ordered at
your local bookshop or are available by post
from Book Service by Post (tel: 01624 836000)

William's Haunted House and Other Stories

Adapted from Richmal Crompton's
original stories by Martin Jarvis

Illustrated by Tony Ross

MACMILLAN CHILDREN'S BOOKS

First published 1999 by Macmillan Children's Books
a division of Macmillan Publishers Limited
20 New Wharf Road, London N1 9RR
Basingstoke and Oxford
www.panmacmillan.com

Associated companies throughout the world

ISBN 0 330 39101 1

Original texts of the stories copyright © Richmal C Ashbee
Adaptations from the original texts copyright © Martin Jarvis 1986–98
Illustrations copyright © Tony Ross 1999

7 9 8

A CIP catalogue record for this book is available from
the British Library

Typeset by SX Composing DTP, Rayleigh, Essex
Printed and bound in Great Britain by Mackays of Chatham plc, Kent

Contents

Dear Reader

Ullo. I'm William Brown. Spect you've heard of me an' my dog Jumble cause we're jolly famous on account of all the adventures wot me an' my friends the Outlaws have.

Me an' the Outlaws try an' avoid our famlies cause they don' unnerstan' us. Specially my big brother Robert an' my rotten sister Ethel. She's awful. An' my parents are really <u>hartless</u>. Y'know, my father stops my pocket-money for no reason at all, an' my mother never lets me keep pet rats or <u>anythin'</u>.

It's jolly hard bein' an Outlaw an' havin' adventures when no one unnerstan's you, I can tell you.

You can read all about me, if you like, in this excitin' an' speshul new collexion of all my fav'rite stories. I hope you have a jolly gud time readin' 'em.

Yours truly

William Brown

William's Haunted House

The Outlaws had discovered that the old house next door to Miss Hatherly was empty.

"I say," said William, "it'd be just the place for a meeting-place, wun't it? Better than the old barn."

"Yes, but we'd have to be quieter," said Ginger, "or else people'll be hearin' us an' makin' a fuss like what they always do."

William knew Miss Hatherly, whose house overlooked the empty house. He had good cause to know her.

Robert (William's grown-up brother) was deeply enamoured of Marion, Miss Hatherly's niece, and Miss Hatherly disapproved of Robert because he had no money and rode a very noisy motorcycle and dropped cigarette ash on her carpets.

She disapproved of William still more and for reasons too numerous to state.

The empty house became the regular meeting-place of the Outlaws. They always entered cautiously by a hole in the garden hedge, first looking up and down the road to be sure that no one saw them.

The house served many purposes besides that of meeting-place. It was a smuggler's den, a castle, a desert island, and an Indian camp.

It was William, of course, who suggested the midnight feast and the idea was received with eager joy by the others. The next night they all got up and dressed when the rest of their households were in bed.

Cautiously, they made their way to the old house and entered it – disturbing several rats who fled at their approach.

They sat around a stubby candle-end thoughtfully provided by Henry.

They ate sardines and buns and cheese and jam and cakes and desiccated coconut on the dusty floor in the empty upstairs room whose paper hung in cobwebby strands from the wall, while rats squeaked indignantly behind the wainscotting, and the moon, pale with surprise, peeped in at the dirty uncurtained window.

They munched in happy silence and drank lemonade and liquorice-water provided by William.

"I say, let's do it tomorrow, too," said Henry as they rose to depart, and the proposal was eagerly agreed to.

Miss Hatherly was a member of the Society for the Encouragement of Higher Thought. The Society for the Encouragement of Higher Thought had exhausted nearly every branch of Higher Thought. But last week someone had suggested Psychical Revelation.

"We must all collect data," said the President brightly.

"What's 'data'?" said little Miss Simky to her neighbour in a mystified whisper.

"It's French for ghost story," said Miss Sluker.

"Oh!" said little Miss Simky, satisfied.

The next meeting was at Miss Hatherly's house.

The "data" were not very extensive.

"I'm afraid I've no personal experience to record," said little Miss Simky, "though I've read some very exciting datas in magazines and such like – but I'm afraid they won't count."

Then Miss Hatherly, trembling with eagerness, spoke.

"I have a very important revelation to make," she said. "I have discovered that Colonel Henks's old house is haunted."

There was a breathless silence. The eyes of the members of the Society for the Encouragement of Higher Thought almost fell through their spectacles on to the floor.

"*Haunted!*" they screamed in chorus, and little Miss Simky clung to her neighbour in terror.

"Listen!" said Miss Hatherly. "The house is empty, yet I have heard voices and footsteps – the footsteps resembling Colonel Henks's. Last night," – the round-eyed, round-mouthed circle drew nearer – "last night, I heard them most distinctly at midnight, and I firmly believe that Colonel Henks's spirit is trying to attract my attention. I believe that he has a message for me."

Little Miss Simky gave a shrill scream.

"Tonight I shall go there," said Miss Hatherly, and the seekers after Higher Thought screamed again.

"I shall go tonight," she repeated, "and I shall receive the message. I want you all to meet me here this time tomorrow and I will report my experience."

"Oh – what a thrilling data it will make," breathed little Miss Simky.

William was creeping downstairs. It was too windy for him to use the pear tree that grew right up to his bedroom window.

He was dressed in an overcoat over his pyjamas, and he held in his arms ten small apples which were his contribution to the feast.

He looked round anxiously. His arms seemed inadequate for ten apples, but he had promised ten apples for the feast and he must provide them. His pockets were already full of biscuits.

He looked round the moonlit hall. Ah, Robert's "overflow bag"! It was on one of the chairs. Robert had been staying with a friend and had returned late that night.

He had taken his suitcase upstairs and flung the small and shabby bag that he called his "overflow bag" down on a chair. It was still there.

Good! It would do to hold the apples. William opened it. There were a few things inside, but William couldn't stay to take them out. There was plenty of room for the apples anyway.

He shoved them in, took up the bag, and made his way to the dining-room window.

The midnight feast was in full swing.

Henry had forgotten to bring candles, Douglas was half asleep, Ginger was racked by gnawing internal pains as the result of the feast of the night before, and William's mind was on other things; but otherwise all was well.

Someone had given William an old camera the day before and his thoughts were full of it. He had taken six snapshots and was going to develop them tomorrow. He had sold his bow and arrows to a class-mate to buy the necessary chemicals.

As he munched the apples and cheesecakes and chocolate cream and pickled onions and currants provided for the feast, he was, in imagination, developing and fixing his snapshots.

He'd never done it before. He thought he'd enjoy it. It would be so jolly and messy – watery stuff to slosh about in little basins and that kind of thing.

Suddenly, as they munched and lazily discussed the rival merits of catapults and bows and arrows, there came through the silent empty house the sound of the opening of the front door.

The Outlaws stared at each other with crumby mouths wide open – steps were now ascending the front stairs.

Suddenly, a loud and vibrant voice called from the middle of the stairs, "Speak!"

It made the Outlaws start almost out of their skins.

"Speak! Give me your message."

The hair of the Outlaws stood on end.

"A ghost!" whispered Henry with chattering teeth.

"Crikey!" said William. "Let's get out."

They crept silently out of the further door, down the back stairs, out of the window, and fled with all their might down the road.

Meanwhile, upstairs, Miss Hatherly first walked majestically into the closed door and then fell over Robert's "overflow bag" which the Outlaws had forgotten in their panic.

Robert went to see his beloved Marion next day to reassure her of his undying affection. She yawned several times in the course of his speech. She was beginning to find Robert's devotion somewhat monotonous.

"I say," she said, interrupting him as he was telling her that he'd made up a lot more poetry about her but had forgotten to bring it, "do come indoors. They're having some sort of stunt in the drawing-room – Aunt and the High Thinkers, you know. I'm not quite sure what it is – something psychic, she said, but anyway, it ought to be amusing."

Rather reluctantly, Robert followed her into the drawing-room where the Higher Thinkers were assembled. The Higher

Thinkers looked coldly at Robert. He wasn't much thought of in high-thinking circles.

There was an air of intense excitement in the room as Miss Hatherly rose to speak.

"I entered the haunted house," she began in a low, quivering voice, "and at once I heard – *voices*!"

Miss Simky clung in panic to Miss Sluker.

"I proceeded up the stairs and I heard – *footsteps*! I went on undaunted—"

The Higher Thinkers gave a thrilled murmur of admiration.

"And suddenly all was silent, but I felt a – *presence*! It led me – led me along a passage – I *felt* it! It led me to a room—"

Miss Simky screamed again.

"And in the room I found *this*!"

With a dramatic gesture, she brought out Robert's "overflow bag".

"I have not yet investigated it. I wished to do so first in your presence. I feel sure that this is what Colonel Henks has been trying to show me. I am convinced that this will throw light upon the mystery of his death – I am now going to open it."

"If it's human remains," quavered Miss Simky, "I shall faint."

With a determined look, Miss Hatherly opened the bag.

From it she brought out first a pair of faded and very much darned blue socks; next a shirt with a large hole in it; next a bathing suit; and lastly a pair of very grimy white flannel trousers.

The Higher Thinkers looked bewildered. But Miss Hatherly was not daunted.

"They're clues!" she said. "Clues – they must have some meaning. Ah, here's a notebook – this will explain everything."

She opened the notebook and began to read aloud:

"Oh, Marion, my lady fair,
Has eyes of blue and golden hair.
Her heart of gold is kind and true,
She is the sweetest girl you ever knew.
But oh, a dragon guards this jewel,
A hideous dragon, foul and cruel.
The ugliest old thing you ever did see,
Is Marion's aunt, Miss Hatherly—
    What?"

"These socks are both marked 'Robert Brown'," suddenly cried Miss Sluker, who had been examining the "clues".

Miss Hatherly gave a scream of rage and turned to the corner where Robert had been.

But Robert had vanished.

When Robert saw his "overflow bag" he had turned red.

When he saw his socks he had turned purple.

When he saw his shirt he had turned green.

When he saw his trousers he had turned white.

When he saw his notebook he had turned yellow.

When Miss Hatherly began to read he had muttered something about feeling faint and crept unostentatiously out of the window. Marion followed him.

"Well," she said sternly, "you've made a nice mess of everything, haven't you? What on earth have you been doing?"

"I can't think what you thought of those old clothes," said Robert. "I never wear them. I don't know why they were in the bag."

"Oh, do shut up about your things," snapped Marion. "I don't care what you wear. But I'm sick with your writing soppy poetry about me for those asses to read. And why did you give her your bag, you loony?"

"I didn't, Marion," said Robert miserably. "It's a mystery to me how she got it. I've been hunting for it high and low all today. It's simply a mystery!"

"Oh, do stop saying that. What are you going to do about it? That's the point."

"I'm going to commit suicide," said Robert. "I feel there's nothing left to live for now you're turning against me."

"I don't believe you could," said Marion aggressively. "How are you going to do it?"

"I shall drink poison."

"What poison? I don't believe you know what are poisons. What poison?"

"Er – prussic acid," said Robert.

"You couldn't get it. They wouldn't sell it to you."

"People do get poisons," Robert said indignantly. "I'm always reading of people taking poisons."

They had reached Robert's house and were standing just beneath William's window.

"I know heaps of poisons," said Robert. "I'm not going to tell you what I'm going to take. I'm going to—"

At that moment, William, who had been fixing his snapshots and was beginning to "clear up", threw the contents of his fixing bath out of the window with a careless flourish. They fell upon Robert and Marion. For a minute they were both speechless with surprise and solution of sodium hydrosulphate. Then Marion said furiously, "You brute! I hate you."

"Oh, I say," gasped Robert. "It's not my fault, Marion. I don't know what it is. Honestly, I didn't do it—"

Some of the solution had found its way into Robert's mouth and he was trying to eject it as politely as possible.

"It came from your beastly house," said Marion angrily, "and it's ruined my hat and I hate you and I'll never speak to you again."

She turned on her heel and walked off, mopping the back of her neck with a handkerchief as she went.

Robert stared at her unrelenting back till she was out of sight, then went indoors. Ruined her hat indeed? What was a hat anyway? It had ruined his suit – simply ruined it. And how had the old cat got his bag he'd like to know. He wouldn't mind betting a quid that that little wretch William had had something to do with it. He always had.

He decided not to commit suicide after all. He decided to live for years and years and years to make the little wretch's life a misery to him – if he could!

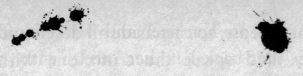

William's Truthful Christmas

William went to church with his family every Sunday morning, but he did not usually listen to the sermon.

But this Sunday, attracted by the frequent repetition of the word "Christmas", William put his stag-beetle back into its box and gave his whole attention to the Vicar's exhortation . . .

"What is it that poisons our whole social life?" said the Vicar earnestly. "What is it that spoils even the holy season that lies before us? It is untruthfulness. Let each one of us decide here and now, for this season of

Christmas at least, to cast aside all deceit and hypocrisy, and speak the truth one with another . . . It will be the first step to a holier life. It will make this Christmas the happiest of our lives . . ."

These words made a deep impression on William. He decided (for this holy season at least) to cast aside deceit and hypocrisy and speak the truth one with another.

He decided to try it at Christmas as the Vicar had suggested.

Much to his disgust William heard that Uncle Frederick and Aunt Emma had asked his family to stay with them for Christmas.

It happened that William's father was summoned on Christmas Eve to the sickbed of one of his aunts and so could not accompany them.

Uncle Frederick and Aunt Emma were very stout and good-natured-looking. They had not seen William since he was a baby.

That explained the fact of their having invited William and his family to spend

Christmas with them.

"So this is little William," said Uncle Frederick, putting his hand on William's head. "And how is little William?"

William removed his head from Uncle Frederick's hand in silence, then said, "V'well, thank you."

"And so grateful to your uncle and aunt for asking you to stay with them, aren't you, William?" said his mother.

William remembered that his career of

truthfulness did not begin till the next day, so he said, "Yes . . ."

William awoke early on Christmas Day. He had hung up his stocking the night before and was pleased to see it fairly full. He took out the presents quickly but not very optimistically.

Yes, as bad as ever! . . . A case containing a pen and pencil and ruler, a new brush and comb, a purse (empty) and a new tie . . . A penknife and a box of toffee were the only redeeming features.

On the chair by his bedside was a book of Church History from Aunt Emma and a box containing a pair of compasses, a protractor and a set square from Uncle Frederick . . .

William appeared at breakfast carrying under his arm his presents for his host and hostess. He exchanged "Happy Christmas" gloomily.

His resolve to cast away deceit and

hypocrisy and speak the truth one with another lay heavy upon him.

"Well, William, darling," said his mother, "did you find your presents?"

"Yes. Thank you."

"Did you like the book and instruments that Uncle and I gave you?" said Aunt Emma brightly.

"No," said William truthfully. "I'm not int'rested in Church History, an' I've got something like those at school. Not that I'd want 'em, if I *hadn't* 'em."

"*William!*" screamed Mrs Brown in horror. "How can you be so ungrateful!"

"I'm not ungrateful," explained William. "I'm only bein' truthful. I'm casting aside deceit an' . . . an' hyp-hyp— what he said. I'm only sayin' that I'm not int'rested in Church History nor in those inst'ments. But thank you very much for 'em."

There was a horrified silence during which William drew his paper packages from under his arm.

"Here are your Christmas presents from me," he said.

The atmosphere brightened.

"It's very kind of you," said Aunt Emma, struggling with the string.

"It's not kind," said William, still treading doggedly the path of truth. "Mother said I'd got to bring you something."

Mrs Brown coughed suddenly and loudly.

"But still – er – very kind," said Aunt Emma, though with less enthusiasm.

At last she brought out a small pincushion.

"Thank you very much, William. You really oughtn't to have spent your money on me like this."

"I din't," said William stonily. "It was left over from Mother's stall at the fête an' Mother said it was no use keepin' it for nex' year because it had got so faded."

Again Mrs Brown coughed loudly but too late. Aunt Emma said, "I see. Yes. Your mother was quite right. But thank you all the same, William."

Uncle Frederick was holding up a leather purse.

"Ah, this is a really useful present," he said jovially.

"I'm 'fraid it's not," said William. "Uncle Jim sent it to Father for his birthday, but Father said it was no use 'cause the catch wouldn' catch, so he gave it to me to give to you."

As soon as the Brown family were left alone it turned upon William in a combined attack.

"I *warned* you!" said Ethel to her mother.

"He ought to be hung," said Robert.

"William, how *could* you?" said Mrs Brown.

During the afternoon there came the sound of a car drawing up. Uncle Frederick looked out of the window.

"It's Lady Atkinson," he said. "Help! Help!"

"Now, Frederick dear," said Aunt Emma hastily. "Don't talk like that and *do* try to be nice to her. She's one of *the* Atkinsons, you know," she explained to Mrs Brown in a whisper as the lady was shown in.

Lady Atkinson was stout and elderly and wore a very youthful hat and coat.

"A happy Christmas to you all!" she said graciously. "The boy? Your nephew? William? How do you do, William?"

She greeted everyone with infinite condescension.

"I've brought you my Christmas present in person," she went on. "Look!"

She took out of an envelope a large signed

photograph of herself. "There now . . . What do you think of that?

Murmurs of admiration and gratitude.

"It's very good, isn't it? You – little boy – don't you think it's very like me?"

William gazed at it critically.

"It's not as fat as you are," was his final offering at the altar of truth.

"*William!*" screamed Mrs Brown. "How *can* you be so impolite!"

"Impolite?" said William. "I'm bein' *truthful*. I can't be everything. Seems to me I'm the only person in the world what *is* truthful an' no one seems to be grateful to me. It *isn't* 's fat as what she is," he went on doggedly, "an' it's not got as many little lines on its face as what she has, an' it's different lookin' altogether. It looks pretty an' she doesn't—"

Lady Atkinson towered over him, quivering with rage. "You *nasty* little boy! You – NASTY – little – boy!"

She swept out of the room.

The front door slammed.

William's family were speechless with horror.

Aunt Emma began to weep. "She'll never come to the house again."

"I don't think she will, my dear," said Uncle Frederick cheerfully. "Nothing like the truth, William . . . absolutely nothing."

A diversion was caused at this moment by the arrival of the post. Among it there was a

Christmas card from an artist who had a studio about five minutes' walk from the house.

"How kind of him!" Aunt Emma said. "And we never sent him anything. But there's that calendar that Mr Franks sent to us and it's not written on. Perhaps William could be trusted to take it to Mr Fairly with our compliments while the rest of us go for a short walk."

William was glad of an excuse for escaping. He set off and finally arrived at Mr Fairly's studio. William handed the calendar to Mr Fairly who opened the door. Mr Fairly showed him into the studio with a low bow.

Mr Fairly had a pointed beard and a theatrical manner. He had obviously lunched well – as far as liquid refreshment was concerned at any rate. He was moved to tears by the calendar.

"How kind! How very kind. My dear young friend, forgive this emotion. The world is hard. I am not used to kindness. If you will excuse me, my dear young friend, I will retire to my bedroom where I have the wherewithal to write a letter of thanks to your most delightful and charming relative. I beg you to make yourself at home here . . . Use my house, my dear young friend, as though it were your own . . ."

He waved his arms and retreated unsteadily to an inner room, closing the door behind him.

William sat down and waited. Suddenly a fresh aspect of his Christmas resolution occurred to him.

If you were speaking the truth one with another yourself, surely you might take everything that other people said for truth?

He'd said, "Use this house, my dear young friend, as though it were your own . . ." Well, he would.

William went across the room and opened a cupboard. It contained a medley of paints, two palettes and a cake.

He attacked the cake with gusto. William felt refreshed. He looked round the studio: a figure sat upon a couch on a small platform.

William approached it cautiously. It was almost life-size, like a large puppet, and clad in a piece of thin silk.

William lifted it. It was quite light. He put it on a chair by the window.

Then he dressed the figure in a bonnet and mackintosh he saw hanging on a peg. He found a piece of black gauze and put it over

31

the figure's face as a veil, and tied it round the bonnet.

He felt all the thrill of a creative artist. He shook hands with it and talked to it. He called it Annabel.

Then he remembered the note he was waiting for. He knocked gently at the bedroom door. There was no answer. He opened the door and entered. On the writing-table by the door was a letter:

Dear Friend,
Many thanks for your beautiful calendar.
Words fail me . . .

Then came a blot and that was all. Words had failed Mr Fairly so completely that he lay outstretched on the sofa by the window, sleeping the sleep of the slightly inebriated. William returned to the studio.

Then he thought of a game. He caught up the figure in his arms and dashed into the street with it. The danger and exhilaration of this race for freedom through the street with

Annabel in his arms was too enticing to be resisted.

As a matter of fact the flight through the streets was rather disappointing. He met no one, and no one pursued him.

He staggered up the steps to Aunt Emma's house still carrying Annabel. There he realised that his rescue of Annabel was not likely to be received enthusiastically by his home circle. And Annabel was not easy to conceal.

The house seemed empty, but he could already hear them returning from their walk.

The drawing-room door was open, and into it he rushed, deposited Annabel in a chair by the fireplace with her back to the door, and returned to the hall. He assumed his most vacant expression.

To his surprise they crept past the drawing-room door on tiptoe and congregated in the dining-room.

"A caller," said Aunt Emma. "Did you see?"

"Yes, in the drawing-room," said Mrs Brown. "I saw her hat through the window."

"Curses!" said Uncle Frederick. "The maids must have shown her in before they went up to change."

"Perhaps she's collecting for something," said Mrs Brown.

William stood at the back of the group with a sphinx-like expression.

They all crept into the hall. Uncle Frederick went just inside the drawing-room and coughed loudly. Annabel did not move. "Good afternoon," he bellowed.

Annabel still did not move. He went up to her.

"Now look here, my woman—" he began.

But at that instant Mr Fairly burst into the house like a whirlwind, still slightly inebriated and screaming with rage.

"Where's the thief? Where is he? He's stolen my figure. He's eaten my tea. Where is he? He's stolen my charwoman's clothes. He's stolen my figure. He's eaten my tea. Wait till I get him!"

He caught sight of Annabel, rushed into the drawing-room, caught her up in his arms and turned round upon the circle of open-mouthed spectators.

"I *hate* you!" he screamed. "And your nasty little calendars and your nasty little boys!"

With a final snort of fury he turned, still clasping Annabel, and staggered down the front steps. Speechless, they watched his departure. Then, no longer speechless, they turned on William.

"William," said Mrs Brown, "I don't know what's happened and I don't *want* to know but I shall tell your father *all* about it *directly* we get home."

Uncle Frederick saw them off at the station the next day. He slipped a half-crown into William's hand.

"Buy yourself something with that. I'm really grateful to you about Lady— Well, I think Emma's right. I don't think she'll ever come again."

That evening, his father's question as to whether William had been good had been answered as usual in the negative and, refusing to listen to details of accusation or defence, he docked William a month's pocket-money.

But William was not depressed. The ordeal of Christmas was over. Normal life stretched before him once more. His spirits rose. He wandered out into the lane.

There he met Ginger. From Ginger's face,

too, a certain gloom cleared as he saw William.

"Well," said William, "'v you enjoyed it?"

"I had a pair of braces from my aunt," said Ginger. "A pair of *braces*!"

William's grievances burst out.

"I went to church an' took what the Vicar said an' I've been speaking the truth one with another an' leadin' a holier life an' well, it jolly well din't make it the happiest Christmas of my life like what he said it would . . . It

made it the worst. Everyone mad at me all the time – I think I was the only person in the world speaking the truth one with another. And they've took off my pocket-money for it. Well, I've done with it. I'm going back to deceit and – and – oh, what's that word beginning with 'hyp'?"

"Hypnotism?" suggested Ginger.

"Yes, that's it," said William. "Well, I'm goin' back to it first thing tomorrow mornin'."

William
and Uncle George

It was William who bought the horn-rimmed spectacles.

He bought them for sixpence from a boy who had bought them for a shilling from a boy to whose dead aunt's cousin's grandfather they had belonged.

William was intensely proud of them. He wore them in school all the morning. They made everything look vague and blurred, but he bore that inconvenience gladly for the sake of the prestige they lent him.

He was wearing them now as he and Ginger walked home from school.

"I can walk like a man with a false leg," said William, and he began to walk along swinging one stiff leg with a flourish.

"Well, I can click my teeth 's if they was false," said Ginger, and proceeded to bite the air vigorously.

They went on together, stumping and clicking with great determination. Suddenly, they both stopped.

On the footpath just outside a door that opened straight on to the street, stood a bath chair. In it were a rug and a scarf.

"Ah! Here's my bath chair," said William. "'S tirin' walkin' like this with a false leg all the time."

He sat down in the chair. The sensation of being the possessor of both horn-rimmed spectacles and a false leg had been a proud and happy one. He wrapped the rug around his knees.

"You'd better push me a bit," he said to Ginger.

Ginger began to push the bath chair, at first

reluctantly but finally warming to his task. He tore along at a breakneck speed.

William held the precious horn-rimmed spectacles in place with one hand and with the other clutched on to the side of the chair. They stopped for breath at the end of the street.

"You're a jolly good pusher!" said William.

He tucked in his rug and adjusted his spectacles again.

"Do I look like a pore old man?" he said proudly.

Ginger gave a scornful laugh.

"No, you don't. You've gotta boy's face. You've got no lines or whiskers or screwedupness like an old man."

William drew his mouth down and screwed up his eyes into a hideous contortion.

"Do I now?" he said.

Ginger looked at him dispassionately.

"You look like a kind of monkey now," he said.

William took the long knitted scarf that was at the bottom of the bath chair and wound it round his head and face till only his horn-rimmed spectacles could be seen.

"Do I now?" he said in a muffled voice.

"Yes, you do now. At least you look 's if you might be *anything* now."

"All right," said William in his faraway muffled voice. "Pretend I'm an old man. Wheel me back now . . . *slowly*, mind! 'Cause I'm an old man."

They began the return journey. William leant back feebly in his chair enjoying the role of aged invalid, his horn-rimmed spectacles peering out with an air of deep wisdom from a waste of woollen muffler.

Suddenly a woman who was passing stopped.

"Uncle George!" she said in a tone of welcome and surprise.

She was tall and thin and gaily dressed.

"Well, this *is* a pleasant surprise," she said. "When you didn't answer our letter we thought you really weren't going to come to see us. And now I find you on your way to our house. *What* a treat for us! I'd have known you anywhere, *dear* Uncle George, even if I hadn't recognised the bath chair, and the muffler that I knitted for you on your last birthday."

She dropped a vague kiss upon the woollen muffler and then turned to Ginger.

"This boy can go. I can take you on to the house."

She slipped a coin into Ginger's hand.

"Now run away, little boy! I'll look after him."

Ginger, after one bewildered look, fled, and the lady began to push William's chair along briskly.

She bent down and shouted in his ear.

"And how *are* you, dear Uncle George?"

William looked desperately round for some chance of escape, but saw none. Feeling that some reply was necessary, and not wishing to let his voice betray him, he growled.

"So glad," yelled the tall lady into the muffler, "so glad. If you *think* you're better, you *will* be better, you know, as I always used to tell you."

To his horror, William saw that he was being taken in through a large gateway and up a drive. He felt as though he had been captured by some terrible enemy.

He couldn't breathe, and he could hardly see, and he didn't know what was going to happen to him. He growled again.

She left him on a small lawn and went through an opening in the box hedge. William could hear her talking to some people on the other side.

"He's *come*! Uncle George's *come*!" she said in a penetrating whisper.

"Oh *dear*!" said another voice. "He's *so* trying! What shall we do, Frederica?"

"He's *wealthy*, Mother. Anyway, we may as well try to placate him. He hasn't changed a bit, though he's dreadfully muffled up. And he's shrunk a little, I think – you know how old people do – and I'm afraid he's as touchy as ever."

"Perhaps you'd better explain to the boys, Frederica . . . ?"

"Oh *yes*! It's your Great-Uncle George, you know – *ever* so old, and we've not seen him for *ten* years, and he's just come to live here with his *male* attendant, you know, taken a furnished house, and though we asked him to come to see us – he's most *eccentric*, you know, simply won't see *anyone* at his own house – he never even answered and we thought he must be still annoyed. I told him the last time I saw him, ten years ago, that if only he'd think he could walk, he'd be *able* to walk, and it annoyed him. Anyway, to my surprise I found him on his *way* to our house this afternoon—"

William had almost decided to risk making a dash for it, when they all suddenly appeared through the opening in the hedge. William gave a gasp as he saw them.

First came Frederica, the tall, agile lady who had captured him; next a very old lady with a Roman nose and a pair of lorgnettes; next came a young curate; next a muscular young man in a college blazer; and last a little girl.

William knew the little girl. Her name was Emmeline, and she went to the same school as William – and William detested her.

His heart sank as they surrounded him. Nervously he pulled up his rug, spread out his muffler and crouched yet further down in his bath chair.

"You remember Mother, dear Uncle George, don't you?" screamed Frederica into the muffler.

The dignified dame raised the lorgnettes and held out a majestic hand. William merely growled. He was beginning to find the growl effective. They all hastily took a step back.

"Sulking!" explained Frederica in her penetrating whisper. "*Sulking!* Just because I told him on the way here that if he *willed* to be well he *would* be well."

47

"Hush, Frederica! He'll hear you!"

"No, dear, he's almost stone-deaf."

William growled again.

The old lady looked anxious. "I'm afraid he's ill. I hope it's nothing infectious! James, I think you'd better examine him."

Frederica drew one of the bashful and unwilling young men forward.

"This is your great-nephew, James," she shouted. "He's a MEDICAL STUDENT, and he'd SO love to talk to you."

The rest withdrew to the other end of the lawn and watched proceedings from a distance.

"Er – how are you, Uncle George?" said James politely. "If I could see your tongue – er – TONGUE – you seem to be in pain – perhaps – TONGUE – allow me."

He took hold of the muffler around William's head. William gave a sudden shake and a fierce growl and James started back as though he had been bitten.

William's growl was gaining a note of savage, almost blood-curdling ferocity. James gazed at him apprehensively, then, as another growl began to arise from the depth of William's chair, hastily rejoined the others.

"I've – er – examined him," he said. "There's nothing – er – fundamentally wrong with him. He's just – er – got a foul temper, that's all."

"It is a case for you, then, I think, Jonathan," said the old lady grimly.

Frederica drew the reluctant curate across the lawn.

"This is your great-nephew, Jonathan," she yelled into the muffler. "He's in the CHURCH. He's looking forward SO much to a TALK with you, DEAR Uncle George."

With a sprightly nod at the horn-rimmed spectacles, she departed. Jonathan smiled mirthlessly. Then he proceeded to shout at William with whispered interjections.

"GOOD AFTERNOON, UNCLE GEORGE – confound you – WE'RE SO GLAD TO SEE YOU – don't think – WE EXPECT TO SEE A LOT OF YOU

NOW – worse luck – WE WANT TO BE A HAPPY UNITED FAMILY – you crusty old mummy – WE HOPE – er – WE HOPE – er—"

He stopped for breath. William, who was enjoying this part, chuckled. Jonathan, with a sigh of relief, departed.

"It's all right," he said airily. "The old chap's quite good-tempered now. My few words seemed to hit the spot."

William watched the group, wondering what was going to be done next and who was going to do it.

Then he saw two maids come round the house to the lawn.

One carried a table and the other a tray on which were some cakes that made William's mouth water, and – oh, scrummy! – there was a bowl of fruit salad.

Then to his horror he saw Emmeline being launched across the lawn to him by Frederica. Emmeline carried in her hand a bunch of roses. She laid them on the bath chair with an artless and confiding smile.

"Dear Great-Great-Uncle George," she said in her squeaky voice. "We're all so glad to see you and love you so much an'—"

The elders were watching the tableau with proud smiles, and William was summoning his breath for a really ferocious growl, when suddenly everyone turned round.

A little old man, purple with anger, had appeared, running up the drive.

"Where is he?" screamed the little old man

in fury. "They said he came in here – my bath chair – where is he? – the thief – the blackguard – how dare he? – I'll teach him – where is he?"

William did not wait to be taught. With admirable presence of mind he tore off his wrappings, flung away his horn-rimmed spectacles and dashed with all his might through the opening in the hedge and across the back lawn.

The little old man caught up a trowel that the gardener had left near a bed and flung it after William. It caught him neatly on the ankle and changed his swift flight to a limp.

"Dear Uncle George," cooed Frederica to the old man, "I don't know what's happened, but I *always* said you could walk quite well, if you liked."

With a howl of fury, the old man turned on her, snatched up the bowl of fruit salad and emptied it over her head—

The next day William met Ginger on the way to school.

"Well, *you're* brave, aren't you?" he said sarcastically, "goin' off an' leavin' me an not rescuin' me nor nothin'."

"I like that," said Ginger indignantly. "What could I do, I'd like to know. You *would* ride an' me push. 'F you'd bin unselfish an' pushed me, an' me rode, *you'd* 've got off."

Just then Emmeline appeared on the road, wearing the horn-rimmed spectacles.

"I say, those is ours!" said Ginger.

"Oh *no!*" said Emmeline with a shrill triumphant laugh. "I found them on our front lawn. They're *mine* now. You ask William Brown *how* I found them on our front lawn. But they're *mine* now. So there!"

For a moment William was nonplussed. Then a beatific smile spread over his freckled face.

"Dear Great-Great-Uncle George!" he mimicked in a shrill falsetto. "We're all so glad to see you – we love you so much."

Emmeline gave a howl of anger and ran

down the road holding her horn-rimmed spectacles on as she ran.

"I say, what happened yesterday?" said Ginger when she had disappeared.

"Oh, I can't quite remember," said William evasively. "I growled at 'em an' scared 'em no end an' I didn't get any tea an' he threw somethin' at me – oh, a lot of things like that – I can't quite remember. But I say" – with sudden interest – "how much did that woman give you?"

"Sixpence," said Ginger proudly, taking it out of his pocket.

"Come on!" said William joyfully. "Come on, an' let's spend it."

Boys Will Be Boys

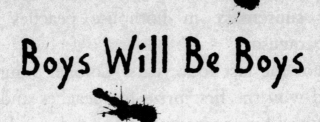

William, much against his will, had been sent to stay with his Aunt Florence.

"I shall be very busy while you're here, William," she said. "I hope you'll be able to entertain yourself."

"Oh, yes," said William. "Oh, yes, I'll be able to entertain myself, all right."

The next morning he sallied forth to inspect the neighbourhood. It was a very small village.

Its chief interest and almost its only topic of conversation was the Flower Show that was to be held at the end of the month.

And that, mainly because of the rivalry of two old men. Of late their rivalry had crystallised into a furious contest for supremacy in hothouse peaches and asparagus.

For the last four years, Colonel Summers had won the first prize for peaches and Mr Foulard for asparagus, and each longed with all his heart and soul to beat the other in his speciality.

This year each had inwardly vowed to win the first prize for *both* . . .

All this William gathered in a stroll round the village.

One afternoon he ran violently into a man just entering a pair of impressive iron gates.

He found himself looking up into the yellow-moustached face of Colonel Summers.

"Well, well, well," said Colonel Summers. "I don't think I know your face, do I?"

"No," said William, scrambling to his feet. "I've come to stay with my aunt."

"Well! Well!" said the Colonel. "You'd better come in and have a brush down. You can't go back to your aunt in that state."

Nothing loath, William accompanied the tall figure up the drive and into the big white house at the end. The Colonel took a clothes brush from the hatstand and gave William a perfunctory brush down, then led him into a room hung round with various Eastern weapons.

"I dare say you'll be interested in these, my boy," he said, and proceeded to describe them in detail, with many somewhat lengthy anecdotes.

William was a most satisfactory audience. He listened open-mouthed. He examined the weapons with eager delight.

He was particularly interested in some Burmese knives in painted leather sheaths.

"Perhaps I'll give you one of those before you go," said Colonel Summers.

He was in high good humour. It was years since he had told the stories except to the accompaniment of strangled yawns. William was a godsend to him.

"Look in again some time," he said

genially, as he saw him off and pointed out a
short cut through the kitchen garden.

"And don't forget, I may give you one of
those knives before you go . . . Shut the gate
after you."

On his way to the gate, William passed a
large hothouse where the famous peaches
were ripening.

In the road he cannoned into someone else.
William became aware of the red, angry face
of Mr Foulard just above his own.

"I hope that'll teach you to look where you're going," he was saying as he administered a number of cuffs. "Disgraceful! Charging into people like that!"

Then he strutted angrily in at a gate that bore the inscription: "Uplands".

The next morning William called on Colonel Summers again. And the next. And the next.

William wanted the Burmese knife, and he shrewdly judged that he was expected to earn it by providing Colonel Summers with an audience.

One morning his footsteps lingered as he passed the hothouse. Today the door was open and the gardener absent . . .

William looked round. The temptation to go in and examine the peaches at closer quarters was irresistible. He went in.

He wouldn't dream of eating any. He stroked one softly.

At least he *meant* to stroke it softly, but to his consternation the stalk snapped and the peach fell on to the ground . . . He gazed at it, at first dismayed, then interested . . .

Well, he might as well *eat* it—

He sank his teeth into the soft flesh. It was *jolly* good. He'd never had anything quite so good.

He looked at the massed peaches all around him. They'd never miss just one more. Actually, he thought, there were far too many. It would be a kindness to thin these peaches a bit.

The best ones hung high overhead, but a ladder was conveniently set up against the top branch. He climbed up . . . took a peach and ate it . . . took another . . . and another . . .

Suddenly he heard a loud shout and the sound of running footsteps. He dropped a half-eaten peach, and looked round.

The gardener and Colonel Summers were running towards the hothouse, their faces livid with fury. Panic-stricken, William slipped, and the ladder went from under him, crashing through the glass.

Instinctively he grabbed at the nearest bough to save himself. There was a shower of peaches and the sound of wrenching as the supports gave way, and the whole tree came down.

The Colonel and his gardener gazed on the scene of destruction, paralysed with horror.

"I don't want to know what happened, William," said his aunt firmly an hour later. "Colonel Summers rang up to ask for your father's address, and I've given it to him. He sounded quite distraught. He's going to write to your father and make his complaint and demand damages. No, I don't want to hear anything more about it. Colonel Summers is going to write to your father."

William decided to go out for a long walk in the afternoon. Passing the gate of Uplands, he saw Mr Foulard smiling at him across the road. William stared at him.

"And how's my young friend?" Mr Foulard was saying.

William scowled, suspecting mockery or a trap, but Mr Foulard was taking some coins out of his pocket, was handing them to William, and saying heartily, "I suppose a little pocket-money never comes amiss? Unless boys have changed since my time, what?"

"Th-th-th-th-thanks," stammered William as he took the two half-crowns.

He couldn't think what had happened since yesterday.

What had happened since yesterday was that Mr Foulard had heard of the destruction of his rival's cherished peach tree, and was delighted by the now certain prospect of winning the first prize for both peaches and asparagus.

"Had tea?" went on Mr Foulard.

William shook his head.

"Come along, then," said Mr Foulard. "Come along!"

He led William up the short drive and in at the door of the house, beaming down at him.

This boy had done (in ten minutes) what he'd been trying in vain to do all these years: knocked out old Summers and his peaches.

"Now we'll see about a piece of plum cake, eh?" he said.

It was while William was just finishing a hearty tea that he got his next shock. Hearing voices outside, he looked up and saw a fat boy and his fat mother passing the window.

"Ah, my daughter and my little grandson,

Georgie," said Mr Foulard. "You haven't met them, have you?"

"Er – yes," said William. "Yes, I've met 'em, all right. I met 'em this afternoon."

"Splendid, splendid!" said Mr Foulard. "I'll go and tell them you're here."

William had indeed encountered the fat Georgie in the street an hour earlier, and had defended himself against Georgie's stone throwing.

William sat staring at the door, a half-eaten piece of plum cake in his hand. Scraps of conversation reached him.

"Not *that* boy!" came in the fat woman's voice. "Not that *dreadful* boy! The one that wrecked poor Colonel Summers' peaches?"

"Boys will be boys," came genially in Mr Foulard's voice. "Boys will be boys, you know. We mustn't be too hard on them."

"And he threw a stone at Georgie."

"Dear, dear!" said Mr Foulard. "That's bad, but – after all . . ." *After all*, he meant, *I shall owe my first prize to him.*

But Georgie's mother brushed him aside and entered the room, fixing a cold stare on William.

"Good afternoon," she said icily.

"Good afternoon," said William.

"You've finished your tea, haven't you?" said Georgie's mother. "I'm sure it's time you went home."

"All right," said William. "All right, I'm goin'—"

He scraped the crumbs on his plate carefully together, put them into his mouth, and withdrew.

Georgie unscrewed his face into a sly smile. He had thought of a plan. Chuckling to himself, he slipped out of the French windows.

William did not hurry. He might as well do a little exploring . . .

He wandered off the drive, took a look at the famous asparagus bed, then began to make his way slowly towards the front gate.

Suddenly a handful of mud struck him on the side of the face, filled his mouth and eyes, and ran down his collar. He had a vision of a fleeing figure and leapt to the pursuit.

Georgie fled as quickly as he could, hardly knowing where he was going, till he reached the asparagus bed. There, William caught him up, and dealt him a powerful blow on the nose that sent him sprawling among the cherished shoots.

Boys in this condition have little sense of property. The two did not even realise that they were fighting on a prize asparagus bed.

They plunged and trampled and leapt and

wrestled. And by the end of five minutes the battleground was a muddy stew, garnished with a few asparagus stalks . . .

When William reached his aunt's house, it was to find that Mr Foulard had rung her up to demand his father's address. He was going to write at once to lodge his complaint and demand compensation for his asparagus bed.

William decided to go out for a walk once more . . .

He encountered Colonel Summers. Colonel Summers had only just received the news of the destruction of his rival's asparagus bed.

"I'm going away till tomorrow. Come in for that knife tomorrow morning. And about that letter . . ."

"Yes?" said William.

"Well, on the whole, I've decided not to send it . . . Boys will be boys . . . Come for your knife tomorrow."

And he went on down the road, leaving William staring after him in amazed relief.

He'd get the knife, after all – and there'd be

only one letter of complaint to his father instead of two.

And, he assured himself, he'd made things fair. They would get a prize each . . . If nothing else happened, of course . . .

But something else did happen.

William was wandering down the road that evening, his heart full of gratitude to Colonel Summers.

When, therefore, passing the Colonel's house, he saw a red glow through the trees, he thought it best to go and investigate.

Perhaps one of his outhouses was on fire. He could not omit this small service to his only friend.

He pushed the gate open and went to where he had seen the glow. It was all right. It was merely the remains of a garden fire.

Relieved, he went out and home again, leaving the gate open . . .

The news reached Mr Foulard just as he was writing the letter to William's father. Colonel

Summers' asparagus bed had been turned into a ploughed field overnight!

Someone had left the gate open, and twenty-five cattle had apparently danced the hornpipe on it! There was not a vestige of asparagus left!

A slow smile spread over his face. Poor old Summers. Peaches *and* asparagus gone. What a state he'd be in!

He saw in his mind's eye the published results of the show. "Mr H.B. Foulard – Hothouse Peaches – First Prize." And poor old Summers nowhere . . .

He began slowly to tear up his letter to William's father. Boys will be boys, he said to himself. No need to be too hard on the little blighter.

The next morning William made his way to Colonel Summers' house.

The Colonel received William coldly.

He did not know that William was responsible for the wreck of his asparagus

bed, but the wreck of it had brought back his earlier grievance about the peaches.

His mind's eye saw those same fatal words that Mr Foulard's saw: "Mr H.B. Foulard – Hothouse Peaches – First Prize."

"The knife?" he said. "What knife?"

"Th–the knife you promised me," stammered William.

"I think you must have misunderstood me. You can hardly expect me to give you one now."

"Well, I've done all I could to make up," pleaded William.

"What have you done?"

"Well, I came in 'cause I *thought* there was a fire, an' I wanted to put it out for you. I din't know it was only a garden fire when I came in."

Colonel Summers' face turned purple.

"So-it-was-*you*-who-left-the-gate-open?" he said between his teeth.

At that moment the door opened and a housemaid entered with a letter.

Colonel Summers took it, and read it.

It was from the Committee of the Flower Show, saying that, owing to war conditions, the show would not be held this year.

A slow smile spread over Colonel Summers' features. Saved! Saved at the eleventh hour! He wouldn't get any first prize, but neither would that worm Foulard.

"Well, well, well, well!" he said, smiling down at William. "What was it you came for? A knife, wasn't it?"

"Y-y-yes, yes, you said you'd—"

"Of course, of course," said the genial Colonel Summers. (Little devil, of course, but so were all boys. Boys will be boys. Poor old Foulard. Ha, ha! Poor old Foulard!)

"Now you can take your choice, my boy, I'll give you any one of them you like—"

It was the evening of William's return. He had gone upstairs to wash after the journey. Mr and Mrs Brown were sitting downstairs waiting for him.

"Odd those letters we had from Florence," said Mr Brown, "saying that William had done something dreadful, and that I should shortly be receiving appalling bills for damages from a Colonel Summers and a Mr Foulard."

At this point William entered. He looked shiningly clean and innocent.

"Well, did you have a nice time at your aunt's?" said Mrs Brown.

"Yes, thanks," said William.

"Anything – er – interesting happen?" said Mr Brown.

William considered.

"No. Nothin' really int'restin'."

"Let me see," said Mr Brown thoughtfully, "there was a Mr Foulard there, wasn't there? Did you have anything to do with him?"

William looked at his father impassively.

"Him?" he said, as if searching in the recesses of his memory. "Oh, yes. He gave me five shillin's an' invited me to tea."

"Oh, and what about – er – Colonel Summers?" said Mrs Brown.

William brought the Burmese knife out of his pocket.

"Yes, he was jolly nice, too. He gave me this."

Mr and Mrs Brown looked at each other and shrugged helplessly.

Meet Just William
Richmal Crompton
Adapted by Martin Jarvis
Illustrated by Tony Ross

Just William as you've never seen him before!

A wonderful new series of *Just William* book, each
containing four of his funniest stories – all specially adapted
for younger readers by Martin Jarvis, the famous "voice of
William" on radio and best-selling audio cassette.

Meet Just William and the long-suffering Brown family, as
well as the Outlaws, Violet Elizabeth Bott and a host of other
favourite characters in these six hilarious books.

Richmal Crompton
Just William and Other Animals

"You can't have another dog, William," said Mrs Brown firmly,
"you've got one."
"Well it's at the vet's, an' I want a dog to be goin' on with."

William has a certain affinity with members of the animal
kingdom. In fact, some would say that William is rather like
his furry friends. And he would do anything to help an animal
in distress (unless it's a cat).

Champion of canine causes, defender of innocent rodents,
avenger of bestial wrongs – no tormentor of rats or pups is
safe when William Brown is around . . .

Ten classic stories of William – and other animals.

"Probably the funniest, toughest children's books ever written"
Sunday Times

Richmal Crompton
Just William at School

"School's not nat'ral at all," said William. "Still, I don't suppose they'd let us give it up altogether, 'cause of schoolmasters havin' to have somethin' to do."

School is fertile ground for a boy of William's infinite trouble-making talent. Especially when he'd rather not be there at all. Whether he's feigning illness to avoid a test, campaigning for the abolition of Latin and Arithmetic, or breaking into Ole Fathead's house in pursuit of justice, William brings muddle and mayhem to anyone who tries to teach him a lesson.

Ten classic stories of William at school – and trying desperately to get out of it!

Richmal Crompton
Just Jimmy

"I'm not a kid," Jimmy said stoutly. "I'm seven and three-quarters and four d-days and a n-night."

Meet Jimmy Manning – a boy in a hurry to grow up, especially if it means he can join his brother Roger's gang, the Three Musketeers.

Whether he's waging war on arch-enemies the Mouldies, plotting to catch criminals with his best friend Bobby Peaslake, or fighting off the attentions of the dreaded Araminta, Jimmy's plans are always ingenious, hilarious – and destined for disaster!

First published in 1949 and lost for decades, *Just Jimmy* is a rediscovered classic from the creator of *Just William*.

Collect all the titles in the
MEET JUST WILLIAM series!

The prices shown below are correct at the time of going to press.
However, Macmillan Publishers reserve the right to show new retail
prices on covers which may differ from those previously advertised.

William's Birthday and Other Stories	0 330 37097 X	£3.99
William and the Hidden Treasure and Other Stories	0 330 39100 3	£3.99
William's Wonderful Plan and Other Stories	0 330 39102 X	£3.99
William and the Prize Cat and Other Stories	0 330 29098 8	£3.99
William and the Haunted House and Other Stories	0 330 39101 1	£3.99
William's Day Off and Other Stories	0 330 39099 6	£3.99

All Macmillan titles can be ordered at your local bookshop
or are available by post from:

**Book Service by Post
PO Box 29, Douglas, Isle of Man IM99 1BQ**

Credit cards accepted. For details:
Telephone: 01624 836000
Fax: 01624 670923
E-mail: bookshop@enterprise.net